# ROSES ARE DREAD, VIOLETS ARE BOO!

## A Vampire Valentine Story

# ROSES ARE DREAD, VIOLETS ARE BOO!

## A Vampire Valentine Story

### BY MICHELLE POPLOFF
### ILLUSTRATED BY BILL BASSO

SCHOLASTIC INC.

New York  Toronto  London  Auckland  Sydney

Mexico City  New Delhi  Hong Kong

For Jordan, Elana, and Ronni—I love my nieces to pieces
—M. P.

For my uncles and aunts
—B. B.

ISBN 0-439-26076-0

12 11 10 9 8 7 6 5 4 3 2 1      1 2 3 4 5 6/0

Printed in the U.S.A.
First Scholastic printing, January 2001

# CONTENTS

| | | |
|---|---|---|
| 1. | Too Weird Wanda | 7 |
| 2. | Uncle Vexter Visits | 15 |
| 3. | Whatever Wanda Wants | 21 |
| 4. | Valentine's Day Blues | 26 |
| 5. | The Queen of Hearts | 37 |
| 6. | Vampires and Valentines | 44 |

# Chapter 1
# TOO WEIRD WANDA

Valentine's Day was on its way.
Wanda Doomsday was foot-stomping
mad, mad, mad.
She had planned to have a Valentine's
Day party.
But none of her classmates wanted
to come.

Now the kids in class were busy making
valentine cards.
*I want valentines. I need valentines,*
thought Wanda.

Wanda faked a few coughs and went
to the back of the class to get a drink.
She walked slowly past each desk,
hoping to see her name on a valentine
card.
"Stop sneaking peeks, Wanda,"
Wayne the Pain said.
He covered his cards.
"I bet I'll get the most valentines,"
bragged Buffy.
*I bet I don't get any*, thought Wanda.

Wanda did have one friend in class.
She was Helen Hooper.
Helen's brother Henry was friends
with Artie, Wanda's older brother.

During lunch, Wanda sat next to
Helen.
She poked Helen in the ribs with
her bony elbow.
"I have a funny feeling no one in
class likes me," she said. "What do you
think?"
"Ouch!" said Helen, rubbing her ribs.
"First of all, I think you should quit
poking people. Second of all, the kids
*do* talk about your weird clothes."
Helen touched Wanda's shiny black-
and-red cape.

"You dress like a vampire," she said,
"and your fangs get yucky when you eat
peanut-butter-and-jelly sandwiches."
Helen handed Wanda a napkin.

"Also," Helen went on, "you should quit playing those dumb tricks on people." Wanda's eyes grew wide.

"Who, me?" she asked.

"Yes, you," said Helen. "Who poured glue on Hector's seat so he stuck to the chair?"

"Hector's stuck-up anyway," Wanda said.

"Remember the daisy pin you wore that squirted water in Wayne's face?"

"Wayne's a pain," said Wanda.

"How about the time you hid a worm
in Buffy's desk?"
Wanda burst out in giggles.
"Buffy's a good screamer. Everyone
laughed."
"Everyone but Buffy," Helen said.
"The kids are tired of your pranks."
Wanda's shoulders drooped.
"I just wanted them to like me," she
said. "Now they just think I'm weird."

# Chapter 2
# UNCLE VEXTER VISITS

Wanda's sad mood lifted when she came
home from school.

Her Uncle Vexter had come to visit!
Uncle Vexter dressed a lot like Wanda
and sent her clothes from his faraway
travels.

He was a pastry chef.

"I'm so glad you're visiting, Uncle Vex,"
said Wanda. "Will you bake us something
special for Valentine's Day?"

"My pleasure," said Uncle Vex. "But
first I've got a riddle for you. What did
the vampire say to the Invisible Man?"
Wanda couldn't guess.
"Long time, no see," said Uncle Vex.
"That's a good one," said
Granny Doomsday.

"Don't you have a riddle for me?"
Uncle Vex asked Wanda.
"Not today. I'm feeling down in the
dumps," Wanda said.
Uncle Vex nodded.
"When I feel that way, I like to pound
on some dough. Let's go into the
kitchen and see what we can do."

While Wanda told Uncle Vex about her problems in school, he showed her how to make heart-shaped cookies. Wanda liked working her fingers through the dough.

"This is fun," Wanda said.

"Don't you feel better now?" asked Uncle Vex.

"You bet I do," said Wanda. "And I've got a great idea. You can come to my class for Valentine's Day and show everyone how to bake cookies!"

Uncle Vex thought for a moment.

"All right," he said. "Ask your teacher if we can use the oven in the school cafeteria."

"Yippee! Yes!" Wanda sang out.

Uncle Vex laughed.

"Now, let Chef Vex show you how to make more valentine treats."

# Chapter 3
# WHATEVER WANDA WANTS

The next day at school, Wanda told the class her big news.

Wanda's teacher, Mrs. Bono, was very pleased.

"You'll see, Helen," Wanda said. "Now the kids will like me. I'm not playing any more tricks. Everyone will get valentine cookies baked by my famous Uncle Vex and me, me, me!" she laughed.

Buffy was right behind her.

"Stop being such a show-off, Wanda," Buffy said.

"I'm not showing off," said Wanda.

"How come we never heard of your
famous uncle before?" Wayne the Pain
asked.

Wanda gulped.

"Uncle Vex travels all over the place,"
she said. "Right now he's visiting us and
is teaching me to bake."

"Sure," said Buffy. "Does he look like you? Is he a real vampire?"

"I bet he won't show up at school," said Hector.

"Maybe he only comes out at night," Wayne the Pain said, howling with laughter.

23

Wanda stomped her foot.

Somehow it landed on Wayne's toe.

"Ouch! Watch it, Wanda."

Now Wayne was howling in pain.

"Whoops! So sorry, Wayne," Wanda said.

"My Uncle Vex will so come to school.

Just wait and see."

When the kids walked away, Wanda looked at Helen.

"What if something goes wrong?" she whispered.

"Don't be such a worrywart, Wanda." Helen patted her shoulder. "What could go wrong?"

# Chapter 4
# VALENTINE'S DAY BLUES

The next morning Wanda woke up
bright and early.

Her shiny black cape was decorated
with red hearts.

Wanda and Artie had breakfast with
Granny.

"Is Uncle Vex awake yet?" Wanda asked.

"Not yet," said Granny Doomsday.

"The poor dear needs his rest. He's been
working so hard. He stays up most of the
night and sleeps late each day."

"I hope he slept well," said Wanda.

"Today's our big—"

Wanda didn't get to finish her sentence
or her breakfast.
A loud crash came from upstairs.
"*Yeoow!*"

Artie jumped up.

"What was that?" he cried.

Wanda gulped.

"Maybe it was the wind whistling through the windows," she said in a squeaky voice.

Granny Doomsday was already running toward the stairs.

"Is that you, Vexter?" she called out.

Wanda and Artie scrambled up behind Granny.

Uncle Vexter was sitting on the floor in the hallway, holding onto his ankle.

A few feet away from him was Wanda's skateboard.

"No skateboarding allowed in the house, Uncle Vexter," Wanda said.

She tried to smile.

"How many times have I told you to keep your skateboard in the closet?" Granny scolded Wanda.

"Now you've really done it," Artie said. "There's no way Uncle Vex can go to school today."

Two fat tears fell down Wanda's cheeks. "I'm so sorry, Uncle Vex. I'm always messing up."

"Let's get some ice on your ankle to keep down the swelling," said Granny.

"Does this mean you're not coming to school?" Wanda asked.

"I'm sorry, Wanda. Right now I'm in a lot of pain," said Uncle Vex. "Maybe I can come in a few days."

"But Valentine's Day will be over," said Wanda. "Now the kids will never believe me. They'll just think this is another one of my tricks."

Wanda stomped her foot.

Artie backed away.

Granny Doomsday put her arm around Wanda.

"Nonsense, dearie. We've seen you baking these past nights right here in our kitchen."

Artie patted his stomach.

"And we've enjoyed it every night, too."

"That's it!" said Uncle Vex. "You can do the baking right here in your own kitchen. I'll sit and supervise. You can show the kids just what to do."

Wanda wiped at her tears.

She looked at Granny.

"Do you think we could?" she asked.

Granny grinned.

"We'll call your teacher and explain everything. If it's all right, then Mrs. Bono and your class can come on over."

"Superriffic!" said Wanda. "We'll have a Valentine's Day class trip. The kids will be coming here after all!"

# Chapter 5
# THE QUEEN OF HEARTS

Mrs. Bono's class walked up Hollows
Hill to the Doomsdays' house.

"Why did the vampire go to the doctor?"
Hector asked.

"I give up," said Helen.

"Because he was coffin," laughed Hector.

"I wonder if Wanda's uncle really hurt
his ankle," said Buffy. "Maybe it's a trick
to get us into their haunted house."

Wayne pretended to shiver.

"If it is, then I'm out of there, cookies or
no cookies."

Granny Doomsday opened the door and welcomed the class inside.

In the kitchen, Uncle Vexter sat with his foot propped up on a chair.

"We've heard a lot about you and Wanda baking together," said Mrs. Bono.

Uncle Vex nodded.

"Yes, Wanda seems to be a chip off the old bat, I mean block," he said.

Uncle Vex coughed.

"Take it away, Wanda. It's baking time."

While Uncle Vex called out directions, Wanda helped her classmates.

They took turns mixing, pouring, rolling, and sprinkling.

It didn't matter that some hearts weren't cookie-cutter perfect.

Everyone had fun.

When the cookies were baking, Uncle Vex talked about his job.

"Does anyone have any questions?" he asked.

Hector raised his hand. "Why are valentine cookies like a baseball game?"

Uncle Vex couldn't guess.

"Because you need a good batter," said Hector.

Uncle Vex chuckled. "Any more?" he asked.

"How does a ghost eat valentine cookies?" Helen asked.

"By goblin," Uncle Vex said.

His nose twitched.

"I think it's time for us to do some goblin right now."

"All right!" the children yelled.

Granny Doomsday and Mrs. Bono took the cookie trays out of the big, old oven. Delicious smells filled the room.

Everyone ate the warm, crispy valentine treats and washed them down with cold milk.

Before long, every last sprinkle and crumb was gone.

"It's time to go back to school now," said Mrs. Bono. "We have to finish our math and then you can deliver your valentine cards."

The class thanked Uncle Vexter for giving them a Valentine's Day to remember.

Granny waved good-bye to the children.

"Do drop in at the Doomsdays' again," she called after them.

# Chapter 6
# VAMPIRES AND VALENTINES

Before the school bell rang, Mrs. Bono
let the class deliver their valentines.
The children quickly ran from desk to
desk, dropping cards here and there.
Wanda was busy making sure she put
the right card on the right desk.
When she returned to her own desk, she
was surprised to see a pile of cards.
The top card was a drawing of a vampire
saying, "I'm batty over you."
Under that was a ghost card that said,
"Roses are dread, violets are boo!"

One card was signed, "Guess who?" and
another said, "From a secret friend."

Wanda let out a deep breath.
She hugged the cards to her.
*Vampires do get valentines*, she thought.
Wanda smiled as she packed away her
cards.
She couldn't wait to get home and show
them to Granny and Uncle Vex.

That night after dinner, Wanda said
to Uncle Vex, "Knock, knock."
"Who's there?" asked her uncle.
"Olive," said Wanda.
"Olive who?" asked Uncle Vex.
"Olive you," yelled Wanda, giving
Uncle Vex a big, soft hug.
Uncle Vex hugged her back. "Knock,
knock," he said.
"Who's there?" asked Wanda.
"Ivan," said Uncle Vex.
"Ivan who?" Wanda asked.
"Ivan to be your valentine," said
Uncle Vex.
"Ivanna be yours, too," said Wanda.

HAPPY VALENTINE'S DAY
FROM THE DOOMSDAYS